Raja Reagan: Elephant in the Room

The 2020 Election

By: Raj Chauhan

Raja Reagan's RNC Speech Day 4, RNC Cleveland, OH

"Good evening, America I'm Raja Reagan, and I will tell you to vote for Donald J Trump because for close to 8 years now Barack Obama has shown zero credibility for his role as President. He has started a division that is still destroying this Country.

 If you elect Donald Trump, there will be no division but there will be unity. There will be no wars and no division during his Presidency. There will be no crime he will make sure that policing will work and that people that break the law and the victims that are harmed by criminals to get justice.

I have bad news for Barack Obama America is not a Socialist Country, nor America is not a Liberal Nation we are the United States of America and we must act as Americans on November 8 2016 to vote for Donald Trump because if we elect Hillary Clinton then there will be darkness in this Country.

We must preserve, protect and defend the Constitution of the United States of America. Donald Trump knows how to do it and he will show other people what America means to the World. He will not stand with dictators but will stand with democracy. Donald Trump is a good man with morals and values may God be with the United States of America.

There will be no time for games, if Trump is voted into the office of President of the United States of America. There will be hope over fear, and there will be no more wars and darkness. Please elect Donald Trump, God Bless You and God Bless America."

~ Raja Reagan~

Prologue: Trump's Impeachment

President Donald Trump was falsely impeached for obstruction of justice with the Congressional investigation and Abuse of Power for the Russian Dossier by Department of Justice Independent Special Prosecutor, Robert Muller, and his team. President Trump tried to appeal this decision but was unable to prove his innocence which meant that he could not run again for another term, which upset both his base and him. He was falsely accused by most Democrats, and this would be the downfall of him. Donald Trump did resign as President of the United States of America. This would anger Republicans because they loved Donald Trump, and Vice President Pence decided not to run. Therefore, this led to another charismatic Republican to run for office. As time passed, however, President Trump campaigned for Raja Reagan, who had helped him win his presidential election, and his Trump supporters were behind him 1, 000%. This was an exciting time for the political arena.

Chapter 1

Raja Reagan's Announcement That He Is Running for President, April 3, 2019

"My Fellow Americans, I am Raja Reagan and I am running for President of the United States of America.

For over 3 years now, we decided to elect a President that can restore the Constitution of the United States of America and not demonize the Country. Our current President was impeached for protecting the nation from harm's way.

When our congress impeaches the President for defending the Country from harm then that is a problem. Therefore, when they accused our current President for Abuse of Power it was all a lie.

Our President was innocent at the time when all of the darkness happened with Russia gate. He had no ties to Russia. Who benefited from the people believing that he was? The Democrats wasted taxpayers' money and impeded Donald Trump's administration from doing the business of the people that elected him into office.

My dad Ronald Reagan long ago wanted to become our President so that the world would be safe from harm, and Communism would end. We have citizens that embrace that evil philosophy, and we have politicians that ignore this because special interest groups that promote this New World Order and transformation of the United States pay them off.

Well, I have an answer - I will be running for the greater good of this beautiful nation, and my mission is to bring America towards freedom. I will represent people of the United States of America. I will not stand with our enemies, but I will stand with our friends to improve our country both short term and long term.

When I am President, I will make sure that Americans will have limited Government with no civil liberties taken away. I will as President Stand up to tyranny and dictators to remove them from power if they threaten the American way of life. I will ensure peace through strength by increasing our military spending by 50%, and America will continue to be the most powerful and peaceful. If any Nation messes with us, we will take them out.

When I am President, school choice is something that will make our young Americans are successful in the future, and our children will get the best education. We will guarantee that family will be involved in our educational systems.

When I am President, I will make sure that people will have jobs in the United States of America, and I will promise you that we will be energy independent. I refused to accept the notion that the USA would be dependent on the world for our energy resources. We will be making our own oil, and we will have small rust belt town's boom again. I will finish the Keystone XL pipeline that Trump started to build. Russia, Iran and Saudi Arabia will no longer rob us and attempt to control us through their oil supplies. We will dominate this realm.

When I am President, our factories will not go overseas; instead, we will stay here and not go to India, Mexico or China for cheap labor and supplies. We will develop more manufacturing factories jobs and will have worldwide demands for our *Made in the USA* products.   China and India will no longer be the number one exporter to the world.   I will have the lowest unemployment rates that will surpass any of Trump's numbers. We must be players on the world stage again and bring down the communist regime of China, whose number one priority is to suck every nation dry and make them dependent on their products by manipulating their prices and charging huge tariffs on our products. We must have fair trade, or our great nation will fail.

When I am President, I will help our allies and will support any peaceful negotiations between countries to stop senseless wars. We have sacrificed our most precious citizens to countless wars that could have been avoided by smarter negations and deals that benefit our country. We have to stay strong and know what benefits our country the most and not be afraid to ask for it or settle for a something less. Fools that are either bought by the World Economic Forum, George Soros, Builder burg Group, China, have ruined this country – we can no longer allow these elite groups to operate as mobs that hold things over our politicians to intimidate them to do the things that benefits them and continues to divide us all. If we allow these groups to continue to operate and not label them as enemies of the state, we will remain divided as a nation and under their control. We have to get out of this slave mindset and imprison those who for years have been manipulating us all- we will no longer live in this feudal state. We must stand up and say, "No More Globalism or New World Order." We are all independent and free; we will not stand with these Neo-Nazis, Communist, mobsters, pedophiles, human traffickers, and anyone else that is determined to bring down our free nation. We are home of the free and the brave; it will take us all to say no more, and I will lead you in this fight.

When I am President of these great United States of America, I will make sure that our economy is the largest on the world stage, and we will be the number one exporter of goods and energy that will be competitive enough to destroy the hold that China and Russia have on our business owners and consumers. I will offer tax breaks to citizens that start small businesses and offer employment opportunities in their communities. We must make our rural communities and small towns stronger, as they are the backbone of this country; their blood, sweat and tears are what makes this country what it is. Hard work is what will make us a prosperous and healthier nation. We have to change the tides of this tyranny.

I will be a leader of action as POTUS and not just words and speeches, I have faith that Americans are ready to be led by someone that will reinstate this country as a world leader and a first world nation. If we continue on the trend that we are going, our country will be a nation of no law and order and a third world country that anyone can rob and take advantage of our weakness. We deserve to have stability, peace and to be able to enjoy the pleasures of this great nation. I will follow constitution, and we will make sure that all Americans get representation. We will lead this nation into a harmonious triumphant country that I know it can be. May God Bless You, and May God Bless the United States of America.

Chapter 2

Raja Reagan's Early Stages of Campaigning

Let's Make America Greater Again

Let's Make America Greater Again was a slogan that Raja Reagan's father, Ronald Reagan, used in his political campaigns while running for President of the United States of America. Raja wanted to use it again as a campaign slogan to rejuvenate and reignite the spirit of patriotism because he is a nationalist. He, also, wanted to tap into the spirit of his father's dream for this country.

"*Let's Make America Greater Again* means that we will make our nation better and stronger, defending and standing with her in the dark times. We can put the America Dream first because it has a lot to offer."

~ Raja Reagan's Rally, Oct 3, 2019.

Raja Reagan's 2020 Campaign Slogan

Raja Reagan Ad's Against (R) Rudolph Anderson

Raja Reagan vs Rudolph Anderson on Jobs

"When I am President of the United States of America, I will make sure that our jobs stay in America. We will build new factories and will make sure that small town's boom. We will make sure that our rustbelt towns thrive and there is a good quality of life. I will make sure that Washington and our government will not take people's right to work away from them. My opponent, Rudolph Anderson, has talked the talk, but he cannot walk the walk. He has had his chance to create jobs for his constituents in Tennessee, but he wasted his time talking about what he would do and never produced any positive net results. This is where I will step in as President to build new factories and keep our town's booming. I am Raja Reagan and I approve this message (Raja Reagan, Nov 4, 2019)."

Raja Reagan made his own ad against candidate to make Rudolph Anderson look like the worse choice as a candidate. Raja Reagan was honest about what Rudolph Anderson, Republican Canidate from TN, has not done as a Senator and is holding him accountable for his inaction to successfully represent his constituents but rather speaking the propaganda of the lobbyists from wealthy companies that were funding his campaign. Raja Reagan is a man of the people and for the people, funding his own campaign and not accepting money from any company or lobbyist.

Raja Reagan Grassroots Rallies

Raja Reagan Rally on nuclear weapons, Bakersfield, CA, September 20, 2019:

"When I'm President I will make sure that our American soil is protected from countries like China, Iran and Russia. I will ensure that no nation that is our enemy will have a nuclear weapon, nor will I support the Iran Nuclear Deal. We will not give Iran nuclear weapons, nor will we give China any of our nuclear weapons. They have stolen enough technology from us; it would not be in our best interest to never allow them to get their hands on our military weapons. We will make sure that nuclear weapons are gone from this earth, and we will make a law against selling any nuclear weapons to any of our enemies. If any country, organization, or person attempts to do this, they will meet the wrath of the United States military. We will be on high alert for any threat against our lives, liberties, prosperity and the pursuit of happiness; we will destroy them. I do not want to contribute to the destruction of the human race. I am a president of peace through strength and great negotiations. I will work hard as President of the United States of America to stop nuclear weapons at once.

We will, also, stop China, Russia, Iran and North Korea from launching missiles at countries that are our allies. It will stop here and now when I am in office. I will go to the UN Security Council, get their support for this, and address the world that China, Russia, Iran and North Korea will never have a nuclear weapon. I will make this happen as president of the United States of America."

Raja Reagan's 50 States Rally, Nov 4, 2019

"My fellow Americans, I bring to you the dream of American leadership that needs to be preserved during this time, and as your President, all 50 States in this beautiful nation will have their rights protected. I want a lot of the issues to be managed by the states; the federal government does not need to govern on the issues that can be handled at a local level. It is not the federal government's job to tell the states what to do. The voters in each state elect their local and state leaders to serve them and their beliefs; the federal government has more than enough on its' plate to focus on and not take away the power of the people. We will limit the Federal Government's power, and we will protect citizens' civil liberties and rights, if they follow the laws. If they do not follow our law and order or commit serious crimes, then they will be imprisoned. The state of California has abolished the death penalty for no rational reasons; the citizens are planning to appeal this in a grassroots movement that I support. Each state has the right to sentence criminals to the death penalty, and I support this. States should respect our country's amendments and the Constitution because that is how our nation developed into a civilized society. As President, I will make sure that the 50 states are following the US Constitution. Without these laws there will be chaos and no order; we are not a third world county – I will not allow us to become one."

Rally of America

Nashville TN, Dec 21, 2019

"I will make sure that our American Constitution is safe, and we will defend our land from our enemies. We will make sure that America will not be threatened at all times; we are a land of religious freedoms. I will stand with the churches, synagogues, mosques and temples of worship, and I will guarantee that they are open for worship. This is the most important issue that threatens us today; there is an underlying movement in this country to abolish religious freedoms. We need to bring God back into our narrative, as we are one nation under Him. In my America, there will be safety to protect our civil liberties, and, yes, there will be policing. I will never support defunding the police – NEVER!"

"My administration will make sure that people of color are friends with the police, and our goal is that crime will go down in our major cities with more employment opportunities for them and prosperity. I will commit to having an entrepreneur czar to help citizens in under privileged communities have opportunities to get support and development for their small business ideas, which will hopefully develop into a multimillion-dollar company. We must invest in women and minority business owners, so that they can grow their companies and provide jobs for their families, friends and communities. We must encourage any of our citizens that want to create business ideas because that means jobs and money flowing into the economy. We want our people be and do whatever their dreams are and to be abundant in life. From this our nation will get stronger, when its' citizens are free and prosperous without so many federal government regulations and taxes. I will give a tax break to these companies and will hopefully inspire everyone to develop their dreams and produce goods to compete with others around the world."

"We will make sure that our border has redundancy in protection from illegal immigrants that enter this Country illegally. We will make sure that new factories are built in the rustbelt areas and in poor areas in our country. We will make sure that kids go to the school of their parents' choice. I believe in school choice to create an educational system that is top notch for our children. Parents can choose to send their children to public, private and Charter schools that provide the best education for their children."

"Have you ever dreamed of living in America were there will be no abortion? Well, we will crackdown on abortion because it is murder, and God said that life starts at conception. We will honor God's wishes and protect our most innocent lives – the precious unborn babies that are made in the image of Savior."

"We will stand up to tyranny when we see it, and we will end Communist countries, empowering others to fight for their freedoms and fair trade to boost their economies around the world. Yes, we can - America can do it because I have hopes that this great nation will be stronger as ever when I am President of the United States of America."

Chapter 3

Republicans Debate: Raja Wins!

Raja Reagan vs Rudolph Anderson

Raja Reagan (R-CA):

"As President I will make sure that the Government is smaller by reducing the size of power and we will make a law saying that the Government will not spy on or also threaten the lives of our fellow Americans. We will make sure that our small government will preserve, protect & defend the Constitution of the United States of America but we will make sure that our government respects our people."-Raja Reagan

Rudolph Anderson (R-TN)

"As President I will make sure that our government does more and provides for our fundamental American values and we will have a government that does more for our people. We will make sure that our government protects America; I do not support the Patriot Act. This was one of the first steps in transforming our country into tyrannical nation that spies on its' citizens and started to condition them to be all right to give up many of their civil liberties. This had an avalanche effect on the US, and I want to reverse this practice. We will not support any fascist practice like this because our party is no longer the party of the elite Bushes but one for anyone that enjoys freedom."

Raja Reagan vs Alvin Wilson

Military Strength

Raja Reagan (R-CA)

"As your President, I will strengthen and rebuild the nation's military in order to not start a war, but we will use peace through our strengths to solve conflicts and problems. We will build new factories in our small towns so that our Army, Marines, Coast Guard, Navy & Air Force will become one of the greatest in the world which we I will do with my heart and time."

Alvin Wilson (R-NY)

"I will make sure that our Military will go into wars and we will stop the enemies from taking over our allies we will make full decision to fight in combat when our enemies are at the line. We must stop them at the right time and we will not let the Enemies get away with it we will put our might and time to stop our enemies."

Raja Reagan vs Andy McCarthy

Border Security

Raja Reagan (R-CA)

"I will make sure that our border is secured with more border patrol agents and a wall with built in security system to keep out illegal immigrants and drug mules. We will not allow any illegal immigrant, drug mules or cartels to step foot in this precious country that we hold dear. They will fail! ICE agents will deport them immediately. We must make sure that every local and state government works hand and hand with our ICE agents to follow all the laws we have in order to deport them back to where they came from, and they can come back again the legal way. I will not allow any local or state government to work against ICE agents, or they will run the risk of having all their federal funding revoked. We must have law and order in order for our country to succeed and be united as one."

Andy McCarthy (R-MI)

"We will make sure that Illegal Immigrants don't come here illegally which means that we will enforce laws that will keep them out which means that Liberals can complain all they want but they will be deported back to where they came from and this means that people have to come back the legal way. We will make sure that our way of handling Illegal Immigration works and what Trump is doing is right but I will be like Trump and there will be no more Illegals in this Country.

Raja Reagan vs Bob Williams

School Choice

Raja Reagan (R-CA)

"I will make sure that our young children go to schools that their parents deem the best for them. I believe in school choice and competition. Public, private, charter and academies that our kids attend will be put on notice that they will be competing for federal funding and must provide all students with a quality education to match those in Asia and Europe. We can no longer take a blind eye and keep funding schools that are failing our children. In addition, my administration will no longer allow Democratic politicians to take over our school systems; we are also going to make sure that more parents are on the school boards to ensure that families come first. My administration will not allow the liberal agenda with CRT and LGBTQ+ education will not be the focus of our schools. We must not focus on social issues but rather having STEM programs in more schools and continue to only focus on reading, writing, and arithmetic. Leave it to the parents to educate their children on these social issues and religious matters; it is not the role of the government to raise the children but just to provide an education equal to that of other countries in order to set them up for success in the future. "

Bob Williams (R-NE)

"I will make sure that our parents have a say in the education system in America because our Kids deserve a better education system which means we will fund less of our Public Schools and fund other Schools that provide the best education for our Children because if the Public School systems fail than send them to another School instead of throwing money out there if they do zero for our kids we will make sure that all of the money goes to funding for our good schools not poor school districts that fail our students.

Raja Reagan vs Ralph Oldbear

Abortion

Raja Reagan (R-CA)

"I will make sure that Abortion will be abolished because when we take a live from the womb and abort it is murder. We will not allow these planned parenthood center's aborting black babies or other babies of any kind we will sign a law on day 1 saying that if any abortion clinic is open than we will make sure to shut it down and send in the detectives to find out what they are doing to the babies in planned parenthood and we will put the doctors that took that innocent life under arrest and put on trial for their crime against God."

Ralph Oldbear (R-VA)

"I will make sure that all abortion clinics are shut down for good and that no one ever has to suffer the pain that the devil putted out there because we will make sure that no American has to suffer the pain that abortion gives to you. I will work day and night to fight the evils of abortion and we will make sure that people will never suffer the horrors and demonic atmosphere that Abortion has and never the less we will fight it on day 1 and we will take away that right or whatever they call it Abortion Rights a right".

Raja Reagan vs Christio R. Bush

Tax Cuts

Raja Reagan (R-CA)

"When I'm President of this Great Country I will cut your taxes by 50% the National Average. We will make sure that our state has lower taxes, and we will make sure that people live a better life. We will not tax our citizens we will make sure that our American's will never have to move out or leave any state because we will make sure that our tax cuts improve the Schools, Jobs & Industry in this Country we will not allow the Liberal politicians tax our American Citizens when I am President so when I'm President there will be Tax Cuts for all Americans and we will make sure that people can save money for big American dreams come true."

Christio R Bush (R-TX)

"When I'm President of the United States I will make sure that we will Lower Taxes in the United States of America with the Government lowering the standard taxes by 50% like Raja Reagan said but I have a better idea we will make sure that the American People will not pay taxes in America ever again but we will also tax them a little bit for their pay for our Schools, Jobs & Industry"

Chapter 4

Historic Nomination
Super Tuesday

Raja Reagan's Headquarters was full, as people noticed that they might have the first Indian American as the nominee of the Republican Party. They cheered as Raja Reagan defeated Bush, Oldbear, Wilson, McCarthy and Anderson. It was evident in the Republican debates that Raja Reagan crushed them all in the debates and built momentum for his candidacy. He was ahead in all the local and national polls and getting closer to Super Tuesday there was no stopping, Raja Reagan. Raja was getting the delegates he needed to become the first non-white nominee in Republican Party's history; he was popular and seen as a strong candidate with the white voters. People had faith in Raja Reagan, and they knew that he was nothing like Barack Obama. Raja Reagan had the charisma and strength of his father, and it was a new generation of Republicans that had faith in his leadership skills and knew that he was going to change the course of our nation for the better. He would embolden citizens to rise up and have the courage to make changes locally and within their own families to make this country great again and to fight against Tyranny and communism of any kind that would try to divide us all. Raja Reagan was becoming the greatest presidential candidate of all to unite our nation's citizens;

he even won over die hard Republican, the League of African American Conservatives, NOW, and the Evangelical community, which shocked all the pundits. How would they narrate this win and describe this republican candidate that was like no other? They could not pigeon hole him, and that angered them.

Raja Reagan's Super Tuesday Speech:

Tuesday, March 3, 2020

 "My Fellow Americans we have won the nomination of the Republican Party people said well we could not do it well we did. We are Republicans and it is time to get to work for the American people as my professor Caldashian said "That the American dream can dream big as we will move through the skies of America with a big accomplishment" we must knowingly tell one another that America is the land of the free and the home of the brave. Republicans stood up for those ideals and we can do it again under our campaign and my promises is to you that when a Nation is needed a hand than we will make sure that America will have a hand during these times. I want to make sure that I will work every day for the American people and I will share my values to this Country even though during these hard times we will not forget those who fought and died to keep our freedoms alive. As President, I will make sure that our American democracy is preserved, protected and defended. We will not allow any of George Washington's principles be destroyed instead we are going to protect them like real Americans. A party that abolished slavery and fought for America has nominated someone new into the party a person that is the adapted of Ronald Reagan and is the sunny days of this Country are about to come ahead as we will make great strides in our Nation and we will make sure that our American generation works and accepts this, Nation America. Our America shines on a city hill and we will not take any of that away, My Fellow Americans the Republican Party has shined. God Bless You and God Bless the Great United States of America."

~Raja Reagan~

The Campaign of America

 After Raja Reagan was officially the Republican candidate for President of the United States, he started to unite and excite his base and the entire conservative, independent, and some ex-liberal voters as the first Non-White nominee to run for office. Most voters had been saturated with talk but no action to back it up, but Raja Reagan's work ethics, values and years of experience in the military, movie acting, volunteer work, and the media demonstrated that he was a man of the people and could serve them to lead them into becoming an unstoppable first world nation. Raja Reagan also told his voters "You have to live by your values," which he demonstrated as his years volunteering to make his community better in Los Angeles, CA, ever since he was in high school and with his military service during the Vietnam War. He wanted all Americans to know that he would build up this Country and its' citizens that he loved so much, which he would talk about in his speeches across the nation. He wanted to reach those that were in rural areas that often are left out of the narrative and discussion of many campaigns, but he knew that this population was truly the backbone of this nation and exemplified all that he talked about in his charismatic speeches. Raja Reagan's popularity and numbers in the national polls were gaining on his opponent, Juliette Carter, who was his Democratic opponent, because he attracted new and independent voters. The Republican Party and its' constituents were exhausted of hearing how horrible the USA was and did not want it to move towards Communism, which is all that the Democrats were proposing. They wanted to hear uplifting and patriotic speech, and Raja gained their support by talking about how much he loved patriotic citizens and build up this country into the super power that it once was. You could always hear young, old, black, brown, Hispanic, Asians, men, women, LGTBQ+, and other subcultures of the population chant his name, "Raja Reagan, Raja

Reagan." He would soon be known be known on social media sites as the Great Amerigipper.

Campaign of America Speech May 4th, 2020

"My fellow Americans, we are going to make a promise that all Americans will be protected when I'm elected President. We will support a Small Government that is for the people and by the people; we will not have Government control our lives. I will make sure to strengthen our Military that will be fierce. We are not going to back down from evil we are going to stand up and defeat evil when we see it in our own backyard. We are not going to allow countries like China, Russia and Iran to cause trouble in our backyard; they will be defeated when I am in office!"

"When I am President, I will support School Choice for our kids. We will allow our parents to have a seat at the table and help to decide what the schools teach. They will have a choice about the type of materials are presented to their children and not be seen as enemies. We will end Teachers Unions' control over pushing the Democratic agenda in the school system to educate the children in the Communistic way of life and glorify it."

 "I will make sure that new jobs and industries are in our small American towns in order to give them a chance to become prosperous and more powerful in order to have more say in how this country is run. Our American farmers are the backbone of this country and some of the wealthiest and hardest workers. We need to teach our 'Generation Z' that through hard work, passion, knowledge of how money can work for them, and education are the keys to breaking the cycle of poverty thinking and just 'making ends meet' in this bountiful Nation. I will start programs and offer grants to inspire entrepreneurs that want to create something and contribute to expanding science, technology, engineering, mathematics, and the arts, so that we can compete on a global stage with Asia and Europe."

"My administration will guarantee that only citizens in this country that need healthcare coverage will have Reagancaid. Reagancaid is a non-government run healthcare program by private insurance companies to ensure that our most vulnerable populations have the best healthcare and run more efficiently, saving the government billions of dollars. Only US citizens will qualify for this program and undocumented immigrants that cross into our borders illegally."

"I want to put term limits to Congressional representatives and not allow anyone and their families and friends to profit from their service to this nation. No other sector in this government serves this country and becomes richer than when they entered into their position. Serving your country is a sacrifice that one is willing to make to uplift and strengthen those that they represent. I will not support a system of corruption and empowering businesses and other countries that have bought their share of control in this country through our congressional representatives. I will not allow our country to be runned by anyone but Americans that are for the people. We will stand with the American dream as George Washington envisioned, ending the suppressive control and colonization from another country. I will make sure that everyone takes advantage of living the American dream like our ancestors did, if they want it bad enough."

"We must honor and value the sacrifices that our Veterans made to keep us all free and be known as home of the brave. We will teach our children that our Veterans are to be respected and cared for by making sure that the VA Healthcare Systems have the staff and top of the line medical care and technology to treat them promptly. I will have my Secretary of the VA cut the management staff by half and fill the positions with more frontline staff that will do the job. We must continue to guarantee the promise that President Lincoln made to our Veterans, and this will be a top priority of my administration. We will live in a Nation where they are treated as Citizens and will give them their own guaranteed protected civil rights, which no other President has given to them and is long overdue. I need your help to 'Make America Greater Again!' God Bless You and God Bless America."

Chapter 5

Democratic Opponent: Juliette Carter

All about Democrat Presidential Candidate, Juliette Carter:

Juliette Carter was the Democratic Canidate for President of the United States of America, 2020. She was born on July 3rd, 1954, in Atlanta, Georgia. She graduated from Atlanta High School in 1972, at the age of 17. She served in the Navy during the Vietnam War from 1972-1976; she flew through the ranks and was the first woman to become a Navy General in 1976-1981, by President Jimmy Carter, who was her father and fellow shipmate. She, also, was Liberal, and she campaigned against Ronald Reagan in 1984, working on Walter Mondale's presidential campaign. In 1988, she ran for the Georgia's

5th District in the House of Representatives and won the election with a very close race, winning by only 1% of the all the votes. She voted against George H.W. Bush's War in Iraq because she vehemently opposed the U.S. getting involved in the civil war of the Sunni and Shia tribes in that region of the world. She favored negotiating a peace agreement instead.

In 1992, Juliette Carter ran for Senator of Georgia, against (R) Paul Coverdell, and she won. As a Georgia Senator, she supported Bill Clinton's policies, like the NAFTA and the '94 Crime Bill, which is extremely controversial and seemed to be racially biased towards African Americans because more citizens were incarcerated because of this. In 2000, she supported Bill Clinton after his role in the Monika Lewinsky scandal, claiming it was nothing more than a Right-Wing conspiracy, which was later proven to be wrong. In 2002, she ran for Atlanta's Mayor and won because she tried to reform the city of Atlanta public schools, which failed and still are still one of the worst school districts in the country. She campaigned on gun control and making Atlanta a safer place to live by defunding the police force even before it was a popular liberal thing to do. Unfortunately, crime rose during her administration by 20%. Her liberal stances on social issues and leadership style were coming in to question by community leaders and local and national pundits. In order to save her reputation in 2006, she decided not to run for a second term and decided to join her parents at the Carter Center running their Peace and Health Programs that her family were known for worldwide.

Even though Juliette Carter dropped out of the political arena in 2006, she still spoke out against George W. Bush on many issues and his right leaning policies. In 2013, she was the second female as Secretary of State under President Barack Obama and was responsible for the negations with the Iran Nuclear Deal. It was later speculated that she coordinated with the Iranians to get unaccounted for millions of dollars transferred to them on a tarmac in Tehran in the middle of the night. Now this is what has been alleged by the Republicans but never investigated or substantiated. When President Trump came into office in 2018, he ended this deal and continued to place sanctions on Iran.

In 2016, she campaigned against Trump for Hillary Clinton and was chosen as her running mate in this historic election, which broke a lot of "glass ceilings." Since Hillary was not nominated as President of the United States of America, she decided that this would be the right time for her to run for the Democratic Presidential candidate and ended up winning it on March 3rd, 2020, "Super Tuesday," when all of the others decided to drop out of the race because of her popularity and the momentum that was building around her campaign. It had always been her dream to become the first woman President of the United States of America, and follow in the footsteps of her father, Jimmy Carter, and try to transform this country in to a more peaceful and compassionate place for anyone that wanted to come to the U.S. to live could. Her campaign slogan was "Bringing American Equality & Change."

The Second Woman

Juliette Carter won the Democratic primaries, and she was the second woman to run for POTUS in this party. Hillary Clinton got behind this nomination and supported her campaign both financially and rallied for her at various cities where she could inspire the Democratic base to vote for Juliette Carter. Since Juliette's parents, President Jimmy Carter and First Lady Rosalyn, were still alive, they also helped her with the Southern regions of the country where they were really popular. However, Juliette Carter was too liberal and leftist as seen by the majority of voters; she had an uphill battle to catch up with the popularity of Raja Reagan in the polls. The Democratic Party was confident that Juliette Carter could win because of her progressive stance on social issues and desire to transform the United States of America into a New World Order, which did not appeal to many sectors of the country, who were Nationalists vs. Globalist.

Many of Juliette Carter's donors were of the elite, upper elite, Wall Street and big businesses tycoons that wanted to maintain their power and control and status quo. They wanted to divide the country more along racial lines and continued to push their agendas through BLM, CRT, and Antifa, who were funded by billionaire George Soros, Nazi, Globalist, and he often bragged of rigging elections and destroying countries through civil wars and uprisings by extreme left-wing groups. This only fueled Raja Reagan's passion and patriotism even more, as he knew this was the battle for the soul of this nation.

Juliette Carter's Speech

"I make the wealthy pay their share of taxes and not the lower and middle classes, who are the hard-working people of this country. The rich should not dictate the power structure and inequality that exists in our country. The power should be run by people of this country. America is for the people, and not just the Capitalist or the Republicans in power."

~Juliette Carter~

This upset **Raja Reagan** very much and motivated him to expose **Juliette Carter** for lying and not being honest about who was funding her campaign with her elite donors and did not completely paint an honest picture of the Republican Party. It was the typical Democratic political trick of pretending to be on the side of the working and lower classes, while the Republicans were just interested in maintaining their "power, control, and only represented White elites." However, this could not be further from the truth in this case. The Ku Klux Klan (KKK) was founded in 1865, in the south as a resistance to the Republican Party's goal of establishing equality in all areas of life for Black Americans. Just like today's Antifa and BLM groups it waged it intimidation tactics with White and Black Republican leaders to keep the status quo of that time of White Supremacy and power structure. The KKK supported the Democratic representatives across the USA that wanted to keep White Supremacy in the South.

When **Raja Reagan** brought up this historical fact at his rallies that on the Democratic Party's website it states that it was established in 1920, after they passed the women's right to vote, this angered their base and brought about a lot of violence and intimidation towards the Republican voters. History was repeating itself, and the Democratic Party under the leadership of **Juliette Carter** were attempting to erase history and dictate the false narrative of its' disgraceful origins, like they continue to do now with destroying historical statues and renaming things to fit the left-wing radical agenda. This emboldened Raja Reagan's patriotism even more and gave him the strength to follow his calling to be POTUS for all man and woman kind alike, no matter what their race, creed, color, sexual orientation, gender, or religion. Raja was ready to expose this lie to all his voters through his TV and online campaigns and in his rallies.

Juliette Carter Campaign Speech

 "My Fellow Americans we are going to unite the American people no matter what. We will take the Republican elites in Washington, and make sure that people get a fair share of social and economic justice."

~Juliette Carter ~

Juliette Carter campaigned on progressivism, and this would mean that many Young Democrats would really on board with her campaign and targeted women voters to support the first Women President. Therefore, Juliette Carter's popularity rose with some of the Democratic Party; however, she was not able to capture the heart of American spirit. Juliette Carter was confused as to why her political speeches and rallies were not reflected in her approval ratings and polls. She questioned how she could defeat Raja Reagan and honor the legacy of her father's presidency to keep the hope for the first woman president alive? She thought that maybe she had to become even more radicalized and gain the support of "the Squad." AOC, Rasheeda Talib, Ilhan Omar, and Ayanna Prestly were courted by Juliette Carter, and they came up with the following campaign slogan for her:

Juliette Carter's 2020 Presidential Campaign Sign

Juliette Carter Rally

"As President, I will make sure that everyone will have equality. We will never allow these Right-Wing politicians to take over the country, and I will make sure that Women have their right to choose what they do with their bodies. I will not allow Raja Reagan to take away abortion. As your President, I will stand with the right of a woman to choose and will keep abortion legal."

"I will make a promise to take on White Supremacy, and we will heal the United States of America from Racism and Greed. We will make a law to tackle any racism in America for the people. As for the Wealthy, I will remove them from power and tax them until they pay their fair share."

"I will stop Climate Change and will eliminate gas cars. We will all be driving electric cars; we must save the planet!"

"Raja Reagan must never become President of the United States of America. I will be the best leader that there has ever been since Barack Obama. I will bring Hope and Change from him, and we will not allow Raja Reagan and his Republicans to take power."

~Juliette Carter April 3th, 2020, Chicago IL. ~

Juliette Carter's Democratic National Convention Speech, Milwaukee, WI, August 20th, 2020

"My fellow Americans, today, we are seeing White Supremacy, Inequality, Capitalism and other backwards injustices weaken our country. We are not going to back down, and I will rise to guarantee that America has equality for all. When I am your President, I will fight for you, and I will make sure that everyone will be welcomed into America. I will not allow Raja Reagan and his Republican friends take over the White House. I have served this Nation far and beyond its' borders in the military. I will carry on the legacy of Hillary Clinton as she tried to be the first female President, and I hope one day that glass ceiling will shatter."

"I will unite all Democrats to stop Republicans from dividing this country. Trump failed the American people, and we have a candidate named Raja Reagan, who has promised to continue many of the failed and oppressive policies of Donald Trump. He plans on taking away national healthcare and a woman's right to choose what they do with their body. Raja Reagan wants to ignore climate change, and he will make America worse again."

"Democrats have worked hard for the American people, and Raja Reagan wants you to think that he is good for the nation but is not. He is conservative and only represents the interests of White and powerful men. I will be a president for all people."

"I will be your President, and I will make sure that America is safe and equal.   I hope to be the Woman Commander and chief that will make everyone feel welcomed into this prosperous country to contribute to my vision of how great we can become under the New World Order. May we bring equality and change to all of our America."

~Juliette Carter ~

 **Chapter 6**

Republican National Convention:

Day 1:

Aryan Caldashian: Former Harvard Professor

"Hello, I am Aryan Caldashian, former Harvard professor, and I want you to vote for Raja Reagan for President. He was always a good student, and when people watched him perform U.S. History musicals and lectured, audiences were mesmerized by his charm and charisma. Also, he led the debate team Harvard to World Championship against Oxford and Cambridge Universities, the toughest teams to compete against."

"Raja Reagan is the right choice for the United States of America, and people need him in office. Democrat Juliette Carter has played the American people with her politics, and it is time for people across this Country to know that if we elected Juliette Carter as POTUS, then our Nation will go down a wrong path. If you elect Raja Reagan, our Nation will be stronger at home and secure. Raja Reagan had the guts to stand for the American people. Raja Reagan is a leader like his adoptive father, the great President

Ronald Reagan, to get the job done and to 'Make America Great Again.'"

"Through Raja Reagan's leadership we will not erase our Constitution, but we will embrace the spirits of our Founding Fathers. We are not Communist China; we are the United States of America. We know that Raja Reagan can lead us from his heart and love for this country, and that is why you should vote Raja Reagan for President."

"Many thanks to all of the people fighting this Covid-19 pandemic and saving lives; we are so blessed to have you! Raja Reagan is a true American Patriot, and we hope that you enjoy him as your leader. God Bless You and God Bless America."

<u>Day 2:</u>

Christio Rosado Bush: Vice Presidential Nominee

"Good evening my fellow Americans. My name is Christio Bush, and I accept the nomination as Vice President of the United States of America. America is first, and my father, President George W. Bush, has always said that I was like my grandfather, the late President George H.W. Bush, because I was inspired by him to take big steps in life. I served my country in 1982, as an officer in the U.S. Navy and wanted to serve as a Patriot. I never gave up, and I kept moving forward and never backed down from my dreams and goals to be a leader."

"As Vice President, I will work with Raja Reagan, and we will make America and the World safe from tyranny and oppression of the terrorist and Communist that threaten our way of living. Our administration will ensure that America is first in any deals that we make with foreign partners. If Juliette Carter is elected as POTUS, there will be a Nation gone down under and the bright shining light on the hill will be no more. She does not know how to lead, and she has no interest in putting America first. Look at what happened to Atlanta when she was their mayor: crime rose and schools continued to be the worse in the nation, leaving our children behind. The only people she cares about putting first are the rich Wall Street and companies that are her main donors who do not pay their fair share in taxes that she is always talking about at her rallies. That's right, America, she wants to make Bill Gates, Jeff Bezos, and Warren Buffett rich again. She will continue to make the rich even richer, while the poor and middle class continue to pay all the taxes that run this country. There is not a racial but a socioeconomic divide in this country. If Juliette Carter is elected, this divide will continue to increase, and you will continue to give away more and more of your civil liberties, as the radical left will dictate to you how will live and what you will inject into your bodies, punishing you if you do not submit to it by taking away your livelihood. The Democrats are a party of intimidation and control to keep the status quo of the elites, not allowing all people to be free and prosperous."

"Juliette Carter is pushing the 'First Women President' narrative and hiding the fact that she will be the First Woman Dictator in Chief of the United States of China. That's right people; China is also funding her campaign. She will choose the interest of China first versus our America first policies. What do you want – Communism to choke this country and destroy your civil liberties, or do you want a party that will put all Americans first? This is the choice that you wonderful Americans will have to make. Do not vote for someone based on their gender identity but on what is best for this country. What is best for this country is Raja Reagan as the next President and Commander in Chief.   I look forward to seeing everyone out there voting for us on November 3rd. God Bless You and God Bless America. "

<u>Day 3:</u>

Maryana Reagan: Neurosurgeon and Wife of Raja Reagan

"My fellow Americans, my name is Maryana Reagan, and I am telling you to vote for my husband, Raja Reagan. I would like to tell you that Raja Reagan is the right choice for America because he is a true Conservative Patriot, and he will put America first. He will make sure that all of our citizens are safe from foreign and domestic powers and terrorist. When Raja Reagan came in and said, 'Look Maryana, if I want to be President, I got to be tough and fit for duty to be the Commander in Chief. His life in service has always been a part of his character, and he instilled this same work ethic to our children, Raj, Mary, Jindal, Niraj, Kristna, D'Souza, Christ, Sharuk, Ariya, Rashina, Alfreado, Juliana and Harronshio. He has often taken them to the worst areas of Los Angeles, and they have all volunteered their time helping the homeless, feeding the poor at the soup kitchen, served in the Civil Air Patrol, and cleaning up the trash and graffiti. They have learned that change only comes from team work, leadership, and service to others. Many of our children are plan on a life of service throughout the world and in the military."

"My husband wanted to run for the office of President of the USA, and I was so thrilled and excited for him. Raja knows that when people are out of line with our country, he plans on putting them in their place, like we have had to do with our children at home. I want people to know that when Raja Reagan is your President, the American people will have freedom, and Communism will end. Raja has always stood with the victims of the Vietnam War as a Veteran in the US Air Force, fighting against Communism in South East Asia. While in Vietnam, he saved POW's and will not allow this country to become Communist."

"Juliette Carter will destroy the country with her liberal and far left-wing agenda.   She will ignore the American Constitution by pushing liberal policies, stacking the Supreme Courts, doing away with the filibuster, passing the Green New Deal, which will destroy our economy and make travel impossible, allowing China to gain more power, keeping abortion legal, and will take us into more wars. Do we want to live in a country under the New World Order, or do we want to continue to live in a free society, where we have religious freedom and civil liberties? We will give up all our civil liberties and freedoms under the Carter Administration, and there will be food and gas lines, just like there were under her father, President Jimmy Carter."

"Do we want to go backwards, or move into the 21st Century where we have Space Force and may be able to one day send people to colonize Mars? Which one appeals to you? You have the choice to make on November 3rd, and I know who I will be voting for; a man of great leadership, spiritual beliefs, intelligence and grace to bring peace and unite this great country of ours. He will bring make our economy Great Again and will improve the educational system in this country to make our children Intelligent Again to compete with Asian and other European students that are excelling and beating us in Science, Technology, Engineering, and Math.   The man that will lead us to this greatness is our future President and Chief Commander that I call my husband, Mr. Raja G. Reagan. God Bless You and God Bless America. "

<u>Day 4:</u>

Raja Reagan: Republican Presidential Canidate

"My fellow Americans, my name is Raja Reagan, and I grew up with a good family, the Reagan's. I learned how to have morality and standards in my life; they gave me the life that my poor immigrant parents from India could only dream having. I want every young person who wants to succeed in this country to have all the opportunities that I had to make their dreams a reality. I plan on doing that with mentorship programs and matching up students with leaders in their fields of interest, so that they understand not only how to do the job but the business side too. We are not teaching our children this in the school system. If any student really wants something, they will be able to learn how money works for them and not to work for money. I want to promote entrepreneurship and producing things in this country, so that we will no longer be dependent on foreign products and be in the mess that we are in with supply chain backlog. We will make it popular to have things 'Made in the USA' again!"

"I want to promote service and volunteerism, which is what my father taught me when I was young. I served in the inner city of LA, picking up garbage and helping out in people's homes. I wanted to make a difference in other people's lives that were less fortunate than my family, and I want to promote this sprit to the youth of our great nation. I want them to put down their phones and get to work in their communities, so that they can connect to human beings that are in need. This will make a huge difference in their lives and will teach them great lessons that they can carry with them throughout their lives. Instead of selfies and getting followers, they will compete to get the most service hours instead."

"I served in the Vietnam War because I did not want to dodge the draft, and I chose to enlist rather than going onto college. I wanted to serve my country that I love and has given me so much. America is the land of the free, and the home of the brave. Many brave women and men have sacrificed and died for this country to keep us all free. I will not stand by and watch their deaths go in vain by the liberal elite, like Juliette Carter and her cronies that want to control Washington and have big government to control people's lives. I will not stand by and watch this happen. I am a man of all the people and not the elite; I cannot and will not be bought. I am my own man and put my money behind this campaign."

"For many years the Democrats have been dividing the country based on race, rather taking a look the real culprit of socioeconomic inequalities. Money is power in this country; it's the haves and have nots, which is truly evident in the judicial system that has rules and punishments that are different for those with money. I want to give every citizen the education, work, and promote them to be in business for themselves, so that they will be the bosses of their lives and choose to have the power to decide how to live their lives, bringing others along with them in the process. Let's make business development popular again! Why should only the elite decide how the rest of us should live? You will have less regulation and fewer taxes to pay, especially if you are employing others and are encouraging your employees to develop their own businesses under my administration."

"When I am your President, I will make sure that our citizens will feel safe expressing their opinions anywhere and on any platform. I will not tolerate anyone from being censored or cancelled; I will protect the first amendment of the Constitution. We as a free country will be more tolerant of each other's points of views, even when we disagree with one another. No student should feel scared or threatened by others in their classrooms if they express an unpopular or politically incorrect idea. We must encourage our young to produce their own ideas and to produce creative solutions to big problems that our world faces. If we silence a thought, we may never know what or how that idea may have given birth to a new way of possibly transforming humanity. What a shame that would be!"

"I will strengthen our military, close the borders, create new jobs, and have school choice. We do not want America to return to the '70's, but we want create a future for our children and grandchildren that is prosperous, strong, and powerful. Our nation will be shining strongly, and in the name of Jesus Christ we pray for the best for people during these times of pandemics and civil unrest. I will lay down the law and order with the National terrorist groups like Antifa, BLM, and KKK that threaten our way of life. Therefore, I proudly accept this nomination as the Republican candidate for Presidency of the United States of America. God Bless you, and God Bless America. "

Chapter 7
Voter Shift

Surpassing Juliette Carter

After the Republican Convention, Juliette Carter's chances of becoming President were diminishing, as Raja Reagan's momentum and popularity were skyrocketing. People liked how Raja held firm on fighting the status quo and put the elites in their place. He took a strong conservative stance on national and international issues, supported the military and was firm on law and order to keep America safe. Most of all he was an America first politician and only held USA's interests in how he prioritized his decisions in deals that he would make as a president. His charisma and charm considerably helped him win over people, even the independents and moderate Democrats that backed him. His strong standing in the polls were a referendum against the extreme left leaning and radical caucus of the Democratic Party. People were tired of the oppressive and cancel culture that were slowly destroying our civil liberties and freedoms that we once had in this country. Raja Reagan's candidacy knew this, and he ignited this political giant and force that Juliette Carter and her elite liberal backers did not know how to control and tame.

The **2020** riots were out of control, and no local or national leaders seemed capable of controlling the situation to make the larger and more liberal city streets safe for small business owners and citizens that lived there. These liberal and George Soros' backed radicalized groups were attempting to destroy the city structures and legal systems of many of the larger cities. They were wanting small business owners to quit and give up, so that the elite could come in and take control of the properties that they vacated; thus, continuing to get richer and increase the socioeconomic division that plagues our country. It looked hopeless for a while until Raja Reagan took a hard stance on these national terrorist groups; he said, "It is time to lay down law and order in our major cities. It is time for our liberal friends to wake up and realize that crime is increasing. These riots are not acceptable, and under my presidency I will not be defunding the police but increasing the support and funding that they will have. Citizens must respect the police force, or they will go to jail. I will not tolerate this cancer spreading its' deceitful propaganda of equality, when they are raising millions of dollars and getting richer. Where are these funds going to? Have black lives really mattered to them? Are the inner cities and ghettos getting any safer? Who is benefiting from these race wars and destruction? Is it producing jobs or prosperity in these communities? I do not think so. Follow the money and reasons for these events occurring. We must call it like it is; BLM, Antifa, and the Sunrise Movement are at their core are only trying to break the American spirit. I will not allow them to break us all. We must stand together as one people with one mission to save our country and the freedoms we all hold dear to the American dream that our founding fathers had for us all. We must not leave a mess for future generations to clean up. This is our mess, and we will all clean it up together until every last political terrorist is in jail and can no longer attempt to kill the spirit and strength of our nation."

People fled the major cities, and this would hurt the Democrats, as Raja Reagan brought to the forefront the increase in crime in mostly liberal cities with defunding the police and allowing the riots to continue all that summer in 2020. People were looking for hope and change that the Democrats preached that they would bring, and they were finding this with Raja Reagan's speeches at his rallies. They no longer had faith in the Democratic Party, which would help Raja Reagan's campaign in the suburbs, as they did not want this crime wave coming their way and changing their lives.

Democrat Juliette Carter only campaigned in the major and more liberal leaning cities, which decreased her chances of her becoming President. Also, she was pushing a narrative of the future of our country that did not appeal to most voters by saying, "It is time to defund the police, and it is time to help black lives that are taken by the police officers. We must not allow police brutality to continue. We will add Social Workers police teams and will limit the type of weapons that they will be allowed to have.   Please know that police should not have authority to kill black people. I support the rioters; I am with them. They are peaceful and are not killing anyone." After she said this, Antifa and BLM members were seen on T.V. burning down businesses and attacking local citizens and police in Portland, OR. Her message was not shared by many of the voters who witnessed what was going on with these movements, and these events definitely did not build backing or trust in Juliette Carter's competency to lead our nation towards something good or different. The "Law and Order" messages from Raja Reagan's campaign were definitely resonating more with the voters, which was reflected in his poll numbers.

The Decline of Juliette Carter

Juliette Carter's numbers declined during the summer, and after the Democratic Convention in Milwaukee, WI. Juliette Carter's Campaign thought it would be a good idea to launch a false conspiracy theory ad that Raja Reagan was born in India, and that he never was raised in the United States of America, turned out to be a lie with his birth certificate proving he was born here, and they tracked down his birth parents, who confirmed this. This racial conspiracy theory would, also, hurt Juliette Carter's reputation and competency to handle race relations, immigration, and her transparency with the voters. Ms. Carter said, "I would tell Raja Reagan and his racist Republicans that we will see equality one day, and that all people are created equally. Democrats do not discriminate, but Republicans do and do not care about anyone. I do not respect Raja Reagan's opinions, and I do not care if my opponent is brown skinned because he does not deserve to be President." These racist statements unnerved a lot of voters, especially people of all color, which left the Democratic Party, giving Raja Reagan an edge over Juliette Carter.

The Rise of Raja Reagan

Raja Reagan knew that he did not focus on race, but he cared about how he would make the USA a better place for the 330 million American citizens, even the ones that would not vote for him. He promised the American people that he would help them during these dark times. Raja Reagan's clear message of how he would lead this country and all its' citizens would change the trajectory of the Nation forever.

What Raja Reagan said about race relations was inspiring to many people: "I do not judge people by the color of their skin but by the content of their character, which is what is most important to us right now. I did not run because I am an Asian American but rather because I care about this country deeply. If I was not a true patriot, I would not have risked my life in the Air Force during the Vietnam War. I saw the worst in person kind there, and I never want our citizens to experience what the communists did to the Vietnamese people. We must all stand against the Neo Nazi terrorist groups that plague us and divide us. We are all human beings, made in the image and likeness of God's love. We must treat one another as such, which is God's Golden Rule." This upset the mainstream media who attacked him for saying that. However, Raja Reagan did not care about what the pundits said about him - he just kept moving forward.

Raja Reagan always campaigned positively and always talked about his mission and direction for this country, which was for more freedom for the American people to develop their dreams and become more prosperous, equaling the distance amongst the socioeconomic classes. Juliette Carter's base and financial backers wanted to stop this message from getting out there to the voters because they wanted to maintain their power and control over the masses, and race was their only way to divide us all. Plus, they did not want to lose control over their wealth and wanted to keep us oppressed and not prosper because this would, also, make the Democratic Party lose voters. Democrats ran under division, oppression, and hatred for Democracy and the American way of life.

Chapter 8 

Raja Reagan vs Juliette Carter Presidential Debate, September 30, 2020

Part One:

Healthcare

Raja Reagan: "Healthcare insurance is a privilege that not all undocumented persons deserve, and it should not be universal and government controlled. American Citizens should be able to make the decision on all aspects of their lives and determine for their families and themselves, if they want it or not.   Like any service, seeing a doctor and receiving their care will cost you, and you will have to pay for it. The Government should not penalize our citizens for not having Healthcare coverage; the Government should stay out of the Healthcare industry. Our Healthcare belongs to the people who want it; we will make sure that this privilege is protected."

 "Under Obama care many people lost their doctors and were offered plans that had a $10,000 deductible to be met. Who got wealthy under Obama care? The insurance companies that were his financial backers because everyone had to have insurance coverage. These plans did not cover much, and the people who bought into the hype of this were left very disappointed and often broke after getting hospitalized or sick. They still had huge bills to cover before the insurance companies would pay for their care. Therefore, they were paying to avoid getting penalized from their government, but the Affordable Care Act was not cheap for many families and left them broke and sick with huge healthcare bills to cover under doctors that they did not choose to have. What kind of gobble gook are we selling here to the American people? They deserve better.”

“However, I think this goes to the bigger picture of the huge divide and gap amongst the different socioeconomic classes; we must push entrepreneurship, education on how money can work for you, and STEM and arts education to encourage our students to produce things to be able to make it on their own and choose the type of lifestyle that they want to have for themselves and their families. “

Juliette Carter: “Healthcare is a human right, and if people who do not have it deserve it. It is a fundamental human right. In a Democratic system healthcare should be available for all, even undocumented immigrants. Our people need to have healthcare coverage, or they will not survive and will go broke when they get sick. This is not right or just. On a daily basis people will die if Raja

Reagan is President because their basic rights of good health will not be covered. "

Economy & Jobs

Raja Reagan: "The economy will grow, if we have lower taxes for the American Citizens and encourage entrepreneurship. I will make sure to have an economic policy that reduces government spending by 50%. We will have a free market for American economics and will encourage competition; we have to get out of the mentality that everyone deserves a reward for their efforts. If people understand money, the tax system and how to grow their wealth through the development of businesses and corporations to protect their assets, we will have less debt and need to spend on things that are not prosperous for our families and our country. Well, when I am President, I will create jobs, and I will build new factories in the rust belt and impoverished areas. These will be places those industries will want to flock to and develop their companies there; it will no longer be called the "rust belt" but more the "Shiny Belt of Prosperity."

Juliette Carter: "I will use the government to spend every dollar that is out there, and I ensure that the federal government create all of the jobs. I will tax the rich to help our economy. I will not allow the rich to have tax breaks because they need to pay their fair share for all people. When I am President, I will bring the jobs back from other countries, and the government will pay for the factories and provide equal pay to all workers. The government will reopen the factories that were shut down. "

Foreign Policy

Raja Reagan: "As President, I will make sure that America stands with our allies, and we will not stand with our enemies. We will end Communist China and other countries that embrace Communism and give them our influence of American Democracy. I will make sure that we make peace through strength with other nations that are our allies and will expand our influence around the world. I will build up our relationship with Israel and other nations to make peace negotiations in order to eradicate every dictator on this planet. Our country will replace them with new presidents that will embrace the American Democracy. I will be a President of America First and will support only those deals that enrich our country. We will be fierce and powerful against countries that are a threat to our way of life; however, we will use this strength to keep us out of unnecessary wars. I do not want to sacrifice anymore of our young men and women's blood on foreign lands that are God awful places to be; trust me, I know through my service with the Air Force during the Vietnam War. I will protect us all from foreign and domestic terrorist groups that would love to see this country crumble under the power communism. I will not allow this to happen under my watch. "

Juliette Carter: "I will make sure that we make peace negations with our allies and our enemies, and we will talk with them. For an example, with Iran, where I was Secretary of State under Barack Obama, I had talks with them and told them that they can have nuclear weapons, as long as they were not threatening other nations in the region. I, also, lifted all sanctions against them. This all fell apart when Donald Trump and the Rhinos got into office and pulled us out of this deal. I had talks with Russia about not threatening the United States of America, and they did not cooperate. Therefore, we had to put sanctions on them, which seemed to work. I helped open relations with China, the Country Raja Reagan hates so much and wants to destroy its' government. Look, when I am President, I guarantee that America will make friends with China and other countries that are seen as a threat to us."

Covid 19 Pandemic

Raja Reagan: "I will end the Covid-19 pandemic and here is how I will do it. First, I will nominate Dr. Joseph Ladapo to oversee the COVID-19 taskforce. Also, I will have the Frontline Doctors have a seat at the FDA and CDC; we need to have everyone in medicine and research represented, so that we can offer the best researched and least invasive methods that are proven to be most effective to help our citizens through this awful sickness. The Frontline doctors recommend when testing positive for, take Hydroxychloroquine and Zinc daily. This protocol is used across the world; India published a study in the White Paper (reference 19). In this example, the National Task for the COVID-19 constituted by Indian Council of Medical Research recommendations for HCQ for prophylaxis of SARS-CoV-2 infection for selected individuals. We must not be behind in research and protocols like this. Also, the data and science do not support quarantines and vaccines, which do not work and do not protect us at all from this virus. We have to pivot from this; it was a good thought, but it is not working. Finally, mask mandates will not be enforced; this does not protect us from the virus.”

“When I am President of the United States, no one will lose their jobs, if they choose not to vaccinate; this must be their choice on what they want to do. There will be no more shutdowns or schools being forced to close; our children lost a couple of years of quality education, social interactions with their peers, and have become more isolative, anxious and depressed. We do not want to lose our citizens to the Mental Health crisis that has plagued us through this crisis. I will ensure that Mental Health care and treatment is more of a focus in this task force to fight this pandemic. I care for people that have Covid-19 and want Americans to feel better. I will try my best of my ability to curve or possibly cure this Covid-19 pandemic."

"China and any government officials, doctors, researchers, pharmaceutical companies, or investors that were involved in the development of the COVID-19 must be prosecuted under Nuremberg trials. I will appointment Rudy Giuliani and Dr. Rand Paul to investigate this more; they will be transparent and will let every citizen know the truth, so that they can make an informed decision on their health approach to COVID-19."

Juliette Carter: "I mandate that everyone is vaccinated; it will be illegal to not be. I will fine citizens and put them in jail, if they do not get their vaccines and booster shots because this is a crime and threatens all of our lives. People will be tested before they go back to school or work. We will have mask mandates because it keeps us safe from Covid-19. In order to keep your job, you must be vaccinated under my administration. I will have AOC oversee all of this and make sure that everyone is compliant with this. We will have people on the streets that will arrest anyone that is not wearing a mask and will ask for their papers to prove that they are vaccinated; they will not be allowed to travel if they do not have this either.”

“We should not blame Asians for this pandemic, like the racist Raja Reagan and his Republican cronies do. I will develop vaccines quickly, and I will make sure that we have teams go door to door and give them to every citizen. We will make sure that all of the money that those big banks have will be paying for the Covid-19 vaccines. I will pay U.S. citizens COVID-19 relief checks while they are quarantined and not working. We need to stay firm while we get control of the spread of this virus; I will be the President that enforces these strict rules. “

Chapter 9

Part 2: **Raja Reagan vs Juliette Carter**

Crime & Gun Policy

Raja Reagan: "I will make sure that crime in our major cities goes down, and I know just how to make that happen. First, we will train anyone that wants to learn how to use a firearm to protect themselves. I will have Officer Brandon Tatum run the taskforce to make gun ownership and safety a priority in this country. I will fund our police and will respect our law enforcement for protecting us and keeping us safe from criminals. However, no Law Enforcement will be funded if it is determined that they are using unnecessary excessive force with criminals that they arrest. I will not allow illegal immigrants with criminal histories and who are drug smuggling to remain in this country; ICE will remove them all and will not be allowed back into our country. I will finish the wall that President Trump started to ensure that we have strong borders to control that enters into our country and to stop crimes from happening, like human trafficking and drug smuggling. Also, we must make our schools safer; every school will have to have metal detectors, locked doors, and armed guards, so that they can stop a mass shooting from happening again.”

“The criminal justice system needs to be reformed too; I will elect Judge Jeanine Pirro and Kim Kardashian to lead a task force to change this and to make it fair for all citizens of every socioeconomic class. We do not want to continue this system of a two-tiered justice system where you can have less of a sentence or shown leniency if you have the money to pay a high-powered attorney. This has to change, and we have to reform the prison system; we must reward communities that offer prisoners avenues to get educations and job training, so that when they re-enter the civilian world, they will be able to survive and not go back to a life of crime. “

“Finally, I want to make Mental Health a priority in schools, families, churches and communities. If someone is at risk for harming themselves or others, we all need to know the signs to get them proper help and treatment. I will have Dr. Stephanie Weiland Knarr lead a taskforce to improve the treatments in place in the USA to look at any cracks to help us better identify where we can make improvements to this broken system. Mental health reform will be a priority under my administration.”

Juliette Carter: “I have our police officers treat people of color with respect, and we will allow them to use excessive force. The police should recognize that Black Lives Matter too. I will have Social Workers on each police force to be able to deescalate situations without using guns or force. We have gun control because no one should be able to have access to lethal weapons; I do not want another mass shooting in schools, like it happened at Parkland and Columbine. We must get the guns off the streets; I will give citizens opportunities to turn in their guns before I get them confiscated through the court system; it will be illegal for anyone that is not in the military or a first responder to own a gun. We cannot allow these guns to be in the United States of America. Also, I do not want another peaceful protestor to be shot like they were in Kenosha. We must do something to stop gun violence. My administration will have the most transformative gun laws in this country to make everyone safer. I will make sure that no American citizen can purchase a firearm because universal background checks and the mental health system have all failed us. We must have extreme reform and change, and I'm the candidate to do this. "

Abortion

Raja Reagan: "Abortion is murder, and it is a crime against God and His children. I can recall reading about how Margret Sanger, the founder of Planned Parenthood, had said, 'We don't want the word to go out that we want to exterminate the Negro population...' She also said, 'I accepted an invitation to talk to the women's branch of the

Ku Klux Klan… I was escorted to the platform, was introduced, and began to speak…In the end, through simple illustrations I believed I had accomplished my purpose. A dozen invitations to speak to similar groups were proffered.'"

"When Democrats say abortion is a woman's right, they support the racial undertone that Margaret Sanger historically set to support the killing of minority babies. No one in the Democratic Party, not even Juliette Carter, have denounced Margaret Sanger's actions and statements. She is glorified for starting Planned Parenthood in inner cities and offering women in these underprivileged communities free or discounted abortions. So, I ask Juliette Carter if she supports Margaret Sanger's statements, or will she openly denounce her here on stage? I know the answer; she will not because she is worried only about losing some female voters. She is complicit and has no backbone to stand against these unjust statements that have tainted our country's past, and she is quick to call Republicans racist. The true racists and oppressors are the Democratic party."

"Abortion goes against God's 10 Commandments of 'Thou shall not kill.' Even the founder of Planned Parenthood called it killing, stating, 'But for my view, I believe that there should be no more babies…The most merciful thing that the large family does to one of its infant members is to kill it.' Which one of my 12 children do you and your liberal cronies propose that I kill, Ms. Carter? This is something she will never answer either. Abortion and Planned Parenthood are all pushing the Eugenics' propaganda to eliminate races and classes of people that Margaret Sanger classified as 'diseased' and saw abortion and birth control as 'weeding out the unfit.'   It is against the law of God to kill the unborn. People should wake up and realize that this is not okay. We are not God, and I thought we had removed the Nazi's during WWII? I guess not; the Democratic Party is supportive of this. Are they the Neo Nazis? We have to start questioning if this is acceptable or not? Which side will you be on? I know; I will be on the side of God and support banning early and late term abortions. We will not fund Planned Parenthood but will shut it down. I do not support the killing of the unborn children of God. "

Juliette Carter: "I guarantee that women have equal access to abortion. Women deserve better, and abortion is not racist. It is a woman's right to choose what she does with her body. It's a woman's body, and no government has the right to tell them what they can and cannot do with their sexual organs. Many women living in poverty have no other choice than abortion; they cannot afford to properly care for their fetus.   If we do not allow abortion to continue, then it would be devastating to see our female citizens suffer and live in pain. The Pro-Life movement is a misguided cause, and the people who follow it are Anti-

Choice. The Pro-Life movement is made up of Bible belt White Males that want to oppress and control women; they are uneducated 'deplorables.' Hillary got it right when she said this. Abortion does not harm people; it is safe at any stage of pregnancy. We will continue to fund Planned Parenthood and all the abortion clinics out there."

Immigration and Opiod Crisis

Raja Reagan: "I think that we should not allow amnesty for Illegal Immigrants. We need to follow the laws that are in place already; people can come legally, like my birth parents did from India. We have processes in place, so that we can vet people and control and know who crosses our borders. I will continue many of the policies that President Donald Trump had in place and will finish the wall. We must know who is crossing our borders to be able to defend ourselves and protect our citizens from violent and dangerous drug cartels and gangs, like MS13. We have an opiod crisis that is plaguing many of our major cities, like Dayton, OH, the overdose capital of the United States. Montgomery County experienced 365 overdose deaths in the first five months of 2017, and 371 in 2016. In the U.S. it is estimated that 44 people die per day from accidental overdose on uploads. This is no longer a matter of time to talk about change; it is a matter of action to end this crisis at the border."

"When I am president, I will put former Arizona Governor, Jan Brewer, in charge of the Department of Homeland Security. We must secure our borders to keep drugs, human trafficking and dangerous criminals from crossing the border. It's a simple concept, and I do not understand how any politician can disagree with this. How is it that the Democrats and Ms. Carter not want to keep us safe? Why do they want the drug cartels to continue to traffic women and children? I thought that the Democrats were Pro-Women; this does not make sense. We must take a hard stance on this. A strong border protects our country too from not having another '9/11' terrorist attack. Ms. Carter, can you tell us who is crossing the border is not a terrorist? Do you know who they are, and what groups they belong to? Voters, I ask you if you want to take a chance with your safety? Will you vote for a candidate that is soft on crime and will risk your safety for votes, or will you stand with me and keep our borders safe? I will finish building that wall."

"Also, we will not give any federal funding to cities that describe themselves as 'Sanctuary Cities.' My administration will give I.C.E. the power to get access to all local databases, so that they know when any illegal immigrant is being discharged from prisons and jails from these 'Sanctuary Cities.' We will send them back to the countries where they came from and will not be allowed to return to the U.S.A. We cannot continue to allow people dying every day from the opioid crisis and violence by illegal immigrants. We must finish the war on drugs that my father's administration started, and I'm the person that will accomplish this in his honor. "

Juliette Carter: "I think we should open our borders, and we should allow refugees come in from war torn countries. We should not allow the Republicans in power to have their war on drugs, and it is not an immigrant's fault for bringing in the drugs. This is a human rights issue; President Trump and Raja Reagan are targeting poor people that just want a better life for their families and themselves. I do not believe in borders. We need a global society, and our country will welcome anyone in that wants to come here."

"I will make sure that people have legal drugs; many illegal substances in the U.S.A. are safe and being allowed in many other countries. I think this will help stop the increase in crime and drug smuggling across our borders, if we make drugs legal. I will stop the opioid crisis by signing into legislation that the government will regulate legal drug businesses and stop the pharmaceutal industry from profiting and pushing these drugs into poor communities. We will have no restrictions on drugs, and I will end the war that Raja Reagan's father started. I am the woman to do it! We will never ignore the opioid today or tomorrow. "

Election Integrity

Raja Reagan: "I will make sure that our elections are not rigged, and we will create law's making elections fair and honest. I will put Mike Lindell in charge of a task force to ensure that all of our elections are fair and balanced, no matter which party is favored in the outcome. If you lose, you lose, but it has to be won fairly. I never allow my children to cheat on tests or their homework, and if they lose in sporting or debate competitions, I have taught them to have good sportsmanship and congratulate your opponent. I will not allow foreign interference in our elections. If you want to vote, then you need a voting I.D. Only legal citizens of the U.S.A. that are law abiding should be able to vote. We cannot allow a criminal to vote in jail because they broke the law, and they need to be punished. Voters need the reassurance that when they cast their ballot, it will not be changed or thrown away; we have to reassure them that every vote counts and matters. Democrats wanted mail voting, but that does more harm than good. Back in my day, we voted in person not by mail, and we should do the same today. Why are dead people voting in mostly liberal cities and multiple times for Democratic candidates? We must get to the bottom of this, and my administration will get the job done right."

Juliette Carter: "I will make sure that everyone and all people have the right to vote. Voting is for everyone, and when the Republicans create obstacles to allow people to do this, then that is a problem. This continues to be about suppressing the minority voters and keeping the poor people from voting. You should not need an I.D. to vote; it should be about being free and equal rules for everyone. We will not allow any Russian spies to steal our elections. It is the American people's votes to decide whether they want a free and fair election, not the Republicans. We cannot allow Republicans to block voting rights. We Democrats want you to have voting rights, and we will make sure that people have those rights to vote. Voting is for everyone and I will make sure that all people have the right to vote. "

Chapter 10

Raja Reagan Historic Win

Breaking News

Raja Reagan has WON! The Election

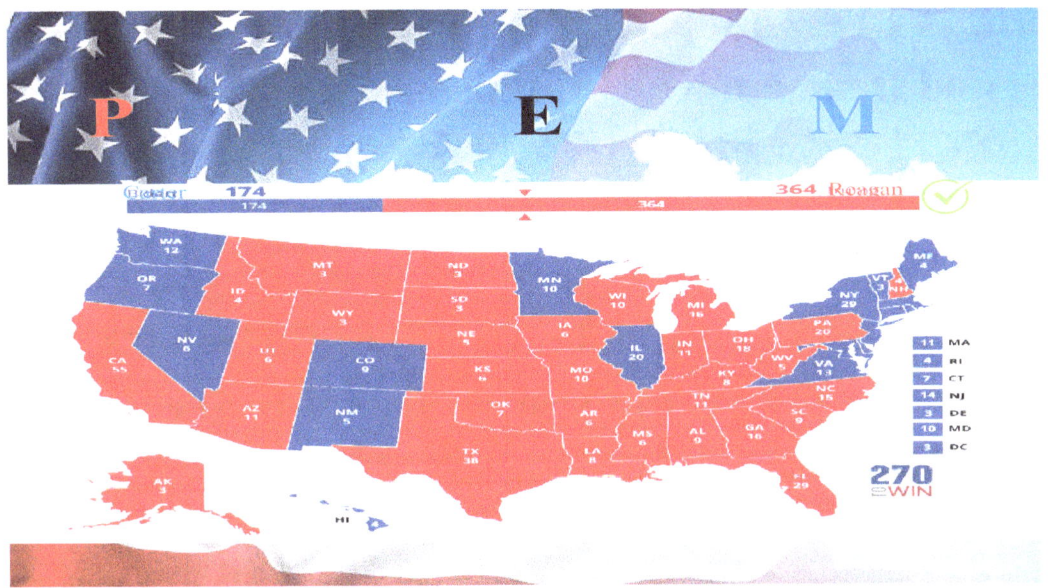

Tucker Carlson, Fox News: "Raja Reagan has won the Presidency of the United States of America. This is historic for the Republican Party and for the United States of America. The first Asian American Conservative ever elected to the highest office in our country has just happened. This is a major accomplishment for a Republican of color. People thought it would never happen, but it did because we can now project that Raja Reagan has carried the State of California, giving him 55 more electoral votes. Therefore, Democrats are disappointed for what has become a new reality. In the end, Raja Reagan won with 364 to Juliette Carter's 174 Electoral College votes. Congratulations America for voting in the right person; thank God. "

Sean Hannity, Fox News: "Raja Reagan is going to Make America Great Again, and we hope for our new President to do what you say you're going to do for this great nation of ours. Raja Reagan surprised the arrogant mainstream media and Democrats by winning tonight, and at the Juliette Carter headquarters there is grief in the air so far. Therefore, our President-Elect of The United States is going to take office on January 20, 2021. This is exciting news for Republicans that have worked their butts off to win the White House. Congratulations, President- Elect Raja G. Reagan."

The California Surprise

California is a traditionally blue state. Nevertheless, when Raja Reagan campaigned hard in California, it turned red. Californian Republicans came out in droves to support their hometown hero and beloved Veteran celebrity, Raja G. Reagan. Raja Reagan won California by winning Los Angeles County and its suburbs; many people that were Latino and Asian's turned out for their candidate Raja Reagan, who did not support a Southern Democrat from Georgia. Raja Reagan knew that winning California, his home state, would give him a boost in the electoral votes needed to win this election. Raja and Ronald Reagan are two of only a handful of Republicans to win the state of California in a presidential election.

Pundits and Democrats never predicted that Raja Reagan would ever win California, but it happened on November 4, 2020. This was an impact that surprised the nation, but it was not a shock to those voters who believed in and supported Raja Reagan every step of his campaign. Why would a liberal California turn red in one election? Well, the answer is the Latino and Asian voters were sick and tired of the high crime rates and progressive policies by Democrats. Plus, in his early years, Raja Reagan volunteered his time in these communities to help them become cleaner and stronger. Raja Reagan never forgot them and kept volunteering his time all his life there with his children, and it paid off big time. His numerous acts of kindness were seen by voters as being endearing and showed that he truly was a man of action and not just words to get votes. Juliette Carter could never match his charisma or the trust that these voters had in him. Raja Reagan won the hardest states for a Republican to win, since George H.W. Bush did in the 1988, presidential election. The 28 years of Democratic stronghold in California was ending.

Juliette Carter's Concession Speech

"My Fellow Americans, I know it was a disappointing finish, but I want President-Elect Raja Reagan to take responsibility for the office as President of the United States of America. Well Democrats, we lost, and this pain will never go away any time soon. We cannot allow a Nation divided, and we will continue to fight for equality, women's rights, healthcare and ending systemic racism. I hope that the next candidate will bring that good fight just I did. We hope that Raja Reagan takes care of the country and does well for the American people. I just was thinking if I was elected President, I would have done many things, but the people have chosen a different President."

"I am proud to accomplish many things, being the first female officer in the U.S. Navy in the 1970's, and the first female General under the Jimmy Carter Presidential administration. Now, I have become the second woman Democratic Presidential candidate that has lost. I know that people will go against our President-Elect, but we should respect the fact that Raja Reagan is the first Asian American President of the United States of America. We cannot just change the results of a free and fair election. However, what we can do next election is to vote for a Democrat that can be better than Raja Reagan."

"Raja Reagan, I have a message for you. I hope you do your best as President of the United States of America, and I hope that one day you succeed for this country. I hope that people trust you and respect you for your term as President. I wish you the best as President of the United States of America. My final message to the American people is we should not go back, and we need to move forward. God bless you all, and God Bless America. "

President-Elect Raja Reagan's Victory Speech

"My fellow Americans, I just called Juliette Carter to say that she tried her best. My fellow Americans, we won for the United States of America, and I pledge allegiance to the flag of the United States of America. Yes, we can get the job done! During these hard times, we must come together and say that we are all America and live in a great Nation with great people. When people settled on this land long ago, they told their children that we are in a new world, and we can survive harsh winters and learned how to be independent by establishing settlements in the Plymouth colony. We are thankful for that event in history, and it is time for our America to continue to grow and shine on a city upon a hill."

"The American dream must never be tarnished, and no one will dare threaten our way of life again under my

Presidency. If they try, we will destroy them and will defeat them. I will remove tyranny from this world, and history will be that America did improve under God with liberty and justice for all by keeping our Constitution at the forefront of all our laws and decisions under my administration. God told us that when America defeats its' enemies, then evil in this world will be destroyed. Our America will carry peace through strength, and we will help the nation recover. It is time for our nation to be healed, and we will continue the dream of President Lincoln when slavery was abolished in 1865. We saw freedom and happiness for people of color, and I will guarantee that those American ideals will be understood by every citizen."

"I wish my dad and mom could be here tonight with us all to share in this great victory. President Ronald Reagan told people at the Berlin wall, "Mr. Gorbachev tear down this wall." The wall came tumbling down, and Communism ended in the U.S.S.R. I will continue my father's fight of ending Communism in every oppressive nation. We must not go back to the days of the Cold War, and we must move ahead to the days of the upcoming Presidency that is about to take place. We will uphold the Constitution for America, and sunny days are coming. God bless you, and God bless America."

~ Raja Reagan Victory Speech, November 4th, 2020

About The Story:

 This book was about a Republican named Raja Reagan, who won the Presidency of the United States of America. It shows that people of color do not have to think or vote for the same Democratic Party, just because they are African American, Asian, or Hispanic. Raja Reagan was an Asian American, but he did not use his race to gain votes because he viewed all people as Americans and cared about is what he could promise to do for them. Raja Reagan wanted to help and care for this country during the darkest of times, after President Donald J. Trump was falsely impeached by the Democratic Party that was in office at that time.

We cover how Raja Reagan rose in the 2020 election by using logical arguments to support his beliefs. He wanted voters to choose him because he was the best choice for the nation. He won the Presidency not because he was Indian, but because had the best and positive vision for this nation. He was the chosen to preserve, protect and defend the Constitution of the United States of America.

I wanted people to read this book because you can see there are Republicans that are Asian Americans and other races too. I want people to understand that our blood is the same color, and we need to treat one another with respect and kindness, instead of dividing us all into classes and races.

Also, I want to see a president that looks like me win in this country; it would be way cool if this would happen.

People can learn from Raja Reagan because he represents us all and the American dream that runs through all of our blood. Instead of cancelling people that have alternative ideas, we need to be able to safely exchange ideas in schools, college campuses, online, etc., because this is still America. I never want to give up my civil liberties and freedom of speech; I do not want America to become like Communist China. We must never let the flames of the dreams of our forefathers and mothers go out and forget those that died for our freedoms. I respect all Veterans' sacrifices to our great nation and will always stand for the National Anthem that symbolizes what unites us all.